There Is a TRIBE of KIDS

LANE SMITH

For Jane Enlow

First published in the USA 2016 by Roaring Brook Press
First published in the UK 2016 by Two Hoots
This edition published 2017 by Two Hoots
an imprint of Pan Macmillan
20 New Wharf Road, London N1 9RR
Associated companies throughout the world
www.panmacmillan.com
ISBN 978-1-5098-1400-8
Text and illustrations copyright © Lane Smith 2016
Book design by Molly Leach
Moral rights asserted

9 8 7 6 5 4 3 2
A CIP catalogue record for this book is available from the British Library.
Printed in China

The illustrations in this book were painted in oils and sprayed with an acrylic
varnish to create various mottled textures. Also used were coloured pencils,
graphite, traditional cut and paste, and digital cut and paste.

www.twohootsbooks.com

There was a TRIBE *of* KIDS.

There was a COLONY *of* PENGUINS.

There was a SMACK *of* JELLYFISH.

There was

a POD

of WHALES.

There was an
UNKINDNESS *of* RAVENS.

There was a FORMATION *of* ROCKS.

There was a

PILE *of* RUBBLE..

There was a GROWTH *of* PLANTS.

There was a

PARADE *of* ELEPHANTS.

There was a TROOP *of* MONKEYS.

There was a
CRASH *of* RHINOS.

There was a BAND *of* GORILLAS.

There was a TURN *of* TURTLES.

There was an ARMY *of* CATERPILLARS.

There was a FLIGHT
of BUTTERFLIES.

There was a SPRINKLE *of* FIREFLIES.

There was a FAMILY *of* STARS.

There was an OCEAN *of* BLUE.

There was a
BED *of* CLAMS.

There was a NIGHT *of* DREAMS.

There was a
TRAIL *of* SHELLS.

There was . . .

a TRIBE *of* KIDS.

There is a

TRIBE *of* KIDS.